Splat the Cat

Storybook Collection

Splat the Cat

Storybook Collection

Based on the creation of Rob Scotton

HARPER

An Imprint of HarperCollinsPublishers

For Nina and Grace Elizabeth

Table of

Contents:

Splat the Cat
Sings Flat

Splat the cat goes to Cat School.

Splat likes to take Seymour.

Seymour is Splat's pet mouse.

Seymour rides in Splat's hat.

One morning,

Splat's teacher had big news.

She asked all the cats

to sit on the big red mat.

Seymour sat in Splat's hat.

"All of you will sing
on Parents' Night,"
Mrs. Wimpydimple said.
"If your singing is loud,
your parents will be proud."

"Will lots of parents be there?"

asked Splat.

"Yes. All the parents,"

said Mrs. Wimpydimple.

"Gulp!" said Splat.

Splat's tail wiggled wildly.

Splat was worried.

Splat was shy.

"I can't sing," said Splat.

"Can you meow?" asked his teacher.

"I forget how to meow," said Splat.

"Can you hum?" asked his teacher.

"I even forget how to hum,"

said Splat.

"That's okay, Splat,"
said Mrs. Wimpydimple.
"I will help you sing.
We will all help you sing."

Mrs. Wimpydimple sang first.

"La-la-la!" she sang.

The cats on the mat began to sing.

All except Splat.

"Now you try, Splat,"
said Mrs. Wimpydimple.
Splat opened his mouth.
Nothing came out.

"You can do it, Splat,"
said his teacher.
Splat tried hard,
but all that came out
was a little squeak.

23

Splat looked at Seymour.

Seymour was brave.

He was a mouse

in a room full of cats.

Splat could be brave, too.

Splat opened his mouth again.

"La!" sang Splat.

The note was loud.

It was long.

And it was very, very flat!

The cats on the mat went wild.

Splat was not trying to be funny,

but he was funny anyway.

"Sing just like that!"
said Mrs. Wimpydimple.
"You will be the star
with a mouse in his hat!"
"Maybe," said Splat.

Splat went home after school.

"What if I forget my part?"

Splat asked Mom and Dad.

"You won't forget,"

they said to Splat.

"Maybe I will forget,"

said Splat.

Splat put Seymour on his head.

Splat's tail wiggled

and Seymour jiggled.

Splat sang "la!"

The note still came out flat.

"Maybe I won't forget,"
said Splat.

Soon it was Parents' Night.

All the parents came

to Splat's classroom.

The class stood on the big red mat.

"Let's begin!" said Mrs.

Wimpydimple.

The class started to sing.

"La-la-la!" sang the cats.

But Splat stayed quiet.

He waited for his turn.

Mrs. Wimpydimple gave Splat a nod.

Splat was ready.

Seymour jumped onto Splat's head.

Seymour was ready, too.

Splat's tail wiggled wildly.

Splat opened his mouth very wide.

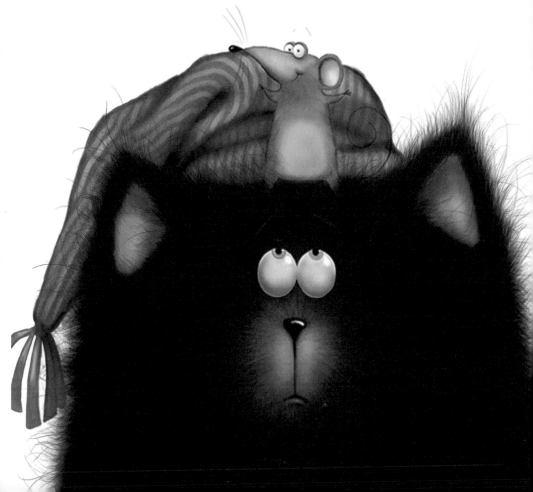

"La!" sang Splat,

and the note was flat.

It was very flat and very loud.

He opened his mouth even wider.

"LA!" sang Splat.

Then he opened his mouth

as wide as it could go.

"LAAA!" sang Splat,
and he fell off the mat.
SPLAT!

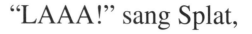

The class giggled.

The parents laughed.

And Splat laughed
the loudest of all.

"You were the star!"

said Splat's mom.

"We are very proud of you,"

said Splat's dad.

"Splat was the cat's meow!"
said Mrs. Wimpydimple.

Splat was happy.

"Guess what," said Splat.

"I didn't forget to sing flat!

I forgot to be shy."

Mom and Dad hugged Splat.

"We love our cat who sings flat."

Splat the Cat

Back to School, Splat!

Splat's tail wiggled wildly with excitement as he walked to Cat School. It was the first day of a new school year, and he could not wait to see his old friends and his teacher, Mrs. Wimpydimple.

Splat's tail dragged behind him as he walked home that afternoon.
Now he was not excited at all.

It was the end of the first day of a new school year, and he already had homework!

"What's wrong, Splat?" asked his little sister.

"I have to do a show-and-tell about my summer vacation," Splat said.

"That sounds like fun," said his little sister.

"But I did so many super things. How can I choose just one thing to show?" Splat said.

Over the summer Splat rode his bike in a very important race.

"Can I come, too?" asked Splat's little sister.
"Little sisters' bikes are not fast enough to race," Splat said.

But she tagged along anyway.

And he went swimming with sharks in the ocean.

"Can I come, too?" asked Splat's little sister.
"Little sisters aren't strong enough to fight off sharks," Splat said.

But she tagged along anyway.

Splat also played in a big soccer game.

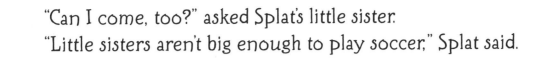

"Can I come, too?" asked Splat's little sister.
"Little sisters aren't big enough to play soccer," Splat said.

sᵤᵣₛₛ S S S S S

But she tagged along anyway.

Splat went searching for pirate treasure.

"Can I come, too?" asked Splat's little sister.
"Finding treasure is too hard for little sisters," Splat said.

But she tagged along anyway.

Splat even built a rocket ship to launch him into space.

"Can I come, too?" asked Splat's little sister.

"Not now!" Splat said. "I'm counting. Ten . . . Nine . . .
Eight . . . Seven . . . Six . . . Five . . . uh-oh . . . I forget what comes next. . . ."

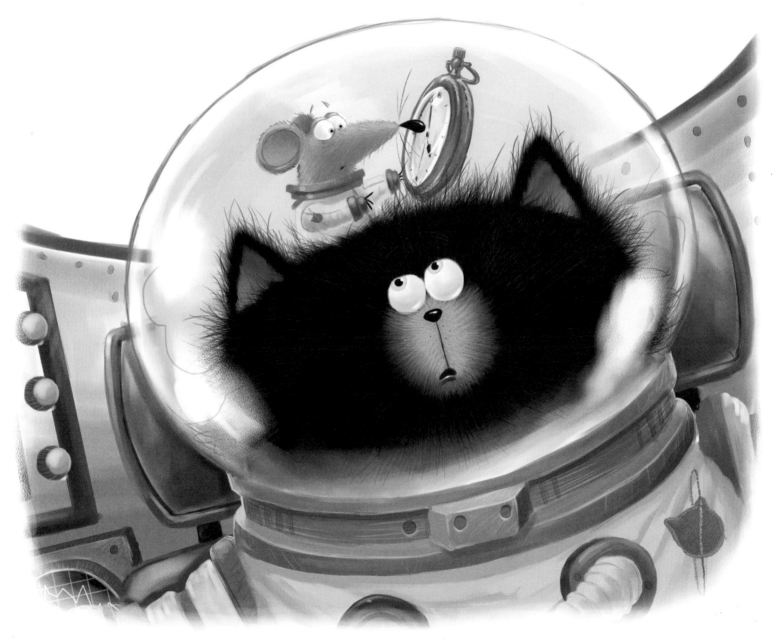

She tagged along anyway.
". . . Four, Three, Two, One, Blastoff!" she said.

"I had lots of adventures," Splat told Seymour. "How can I possibly choose just one thing to show?"

Seymour shrugged. He didn't have any ideas.

Suddenly Splat thought of something.
There *was* one really important thing he could show!

The next day, Splat went to school with his tail wiggling wildly.
And Splat was most pleased that his sister tagged along, too!

Splat the Cat
Good Night, Sleep Tight

Splat was happy.

It was almost night.

He was getting ready

to camp under the moonlight!

"Everything is just right,"
Splat told his mom.
"I have my sleeping bag.
I have my flashlight."

"And I have a surprise,"

said Splat's mom.

"Let's go outside."

Mom and Splat

went into the garden.

They pulled back the tent flaps.

Splat peered inside the tent.

Two sets of eyes peered back.

"Say hello to Spike and Plank,"

said Splat's mom.

"They are camping here tonight!"

Splat felt his whiskers

wobble with fright.

"Mom," whispered Splat,

"I don't like Spike."

"You might like him better

if you spent some time together,"

said Splat's mom.

"You'll see.

Everything will be just right."

"I'm hungry," said Spike.

"What did you bring

for me to eat?"

"I have some fish cakes,"

Splat said.

"Yum," said Spike.

He gobbled them up in delight.

"Look," said Splat.

"The stars are so bright.

I see at least a million."

"I see seventy-one," said Plank.

"I see nothing," said Spike,

"but two silly cats

looking at the moonlight."

"It's getting late," said Splat.

"Let's try to sleep."

But Plank could not rest.

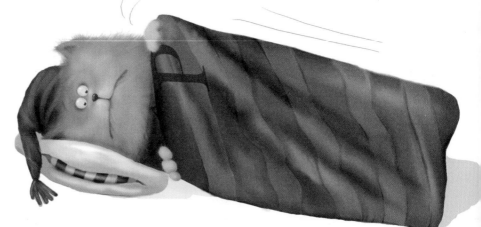

"My sleeping bag

is much too tight," he said.

Plank tossed. He turned.

He struggled, stretched, and strained.

RRRIP!

"You're welcome," said Spike.

Splat was just about to fall asleep

when something felt wrong.

He saw a dark shadow

creep up the tent wall.

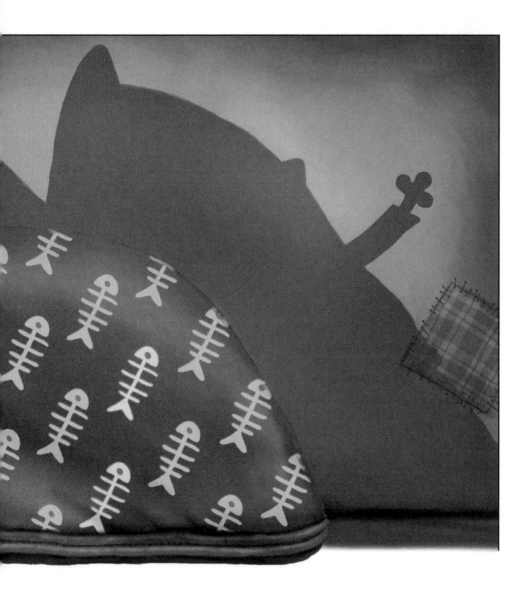

"Run for your lives!"

Splat shouted

with all his might.

SPLAT!

"Oh my."

Spike laughed.

"Did I give you a fright?"

"What's the big deal?" said Spike.

"Everything is all right."

Splat did not think so.

But he was too tired

to pick a fight.

One by one,

Splat's whiskers drooped.

One by one,

his eyes shut tight.

Suddenly, Spike sprang up.

"What's wrong?" said Splat.

"There's something strange

crawling up my leg!" yelled Spike.

"Mommy!" screamed Spike.

He scrambled out of his sleeping bag.

He stumbled out of the tent.

When Spike took flight,
he took the whole tent
down with him.

"Oh, Seymour!" said Splat.

"It was just you."

"It's all right, Spike!

Come back!" said Splat and Plank.

"We will protect each other

for the rest of the night."

"Promise?" sniffled Spike.

"Promise," said Splat.

"Now good night," said Splat.

"Sleep tight," said Plank.

"See you in the morning light,"
said Spike.

For three friends

who camped out that night,

everything turned out just right.

Splat the Cat

The Perfect Present
for Mom & Dad

Splat's tail wiggled wildly with excitement. He wanted to make the perfect present for his mom and dad to show how much he loved them.

"Finished!" said Splat.

But Splat's sister and brother
were making presents, too.

Splat looked at their presents. He looked back at his fish.
It didn't seem so great anymore.

"I can do better!" Splat said suddenly.

"So can I!" said Splat's brother.

"Me, too!" said Splat's sister.

So they all went back to work.

"Look what I made!" said Splat.

Splat's eyes narrowed. So did his sister's and brother's.

"I think I can do even better," said Splat.

"Me, too," said Splat's brother.

"And me," said Splat's sister.

And they all went back to work again.

"Look what I made!" said Splat.

"Look at ours!" said his brother and sister.

"Hmm," said Splat. "I like your kingdom and your jewelry."
"And we like your funny sea creatures," said his brother
and sister.

"I know!" said Splat. "Why don't we make a present together?"
"Great idea," said Splat's brother.
"Yes, it is!" said Splat's sister.

"Now . . . we need something that's as BIG as a kingdom," said Splat's brother.
"As PRETTY as a necklace," said Splat's sister.
"And has lots of FISH," said Splat.

"I know just the thing!" said Splat.

Soon the gift was finished.
"Look what WE made!" they said together.

"Ooh!" said their mom. "A fish tank!"
"Brilliant!" said their dad. "Thank you!"

Mom and Dad weren't the only ones who liked the present.

"Fish! Fish! Fish!" squawked seagulls as they dived into the fish tank.

"That's that, then," said Splat.

Their mom and dad hugged them. "Oh, it's okay," said their mom. "The fish tank was wonderful, but you cats are the best presents of all."

Splat the Cat
and the Duck with No Quack

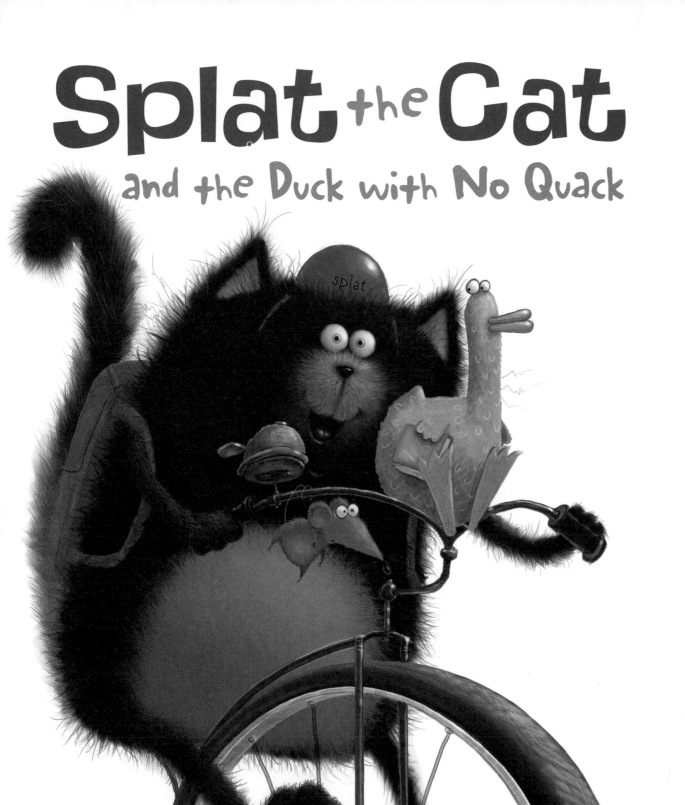

128

Splat's bike went clickity clack
as he rode along a bumpy track
to Cat School.

Suddenly, the wheel of the bike
got stuck in a crack.

With a whack and a smack,

Splat tumbled onto the track.

Splat found himself nose to beak

with a funny duck.

The funny duck had a little book.

The duck gave Splat a funny look.

"How odd!" said Splat.

This duck was strangely quiet.

"A duck lacking in quacking,"

said Splat.

"That's not right!"

"Don't worry, Duck," said Splat.

"You must be lost.

I'll take you back to the pond.

I will help you

get your quack back."

Splat picked up the duck

with the little book

and put both in his backpack.

"Take care in there," said Splat.

"And don't sit on

my fish-stick snack."

Splat put his backpack back on,
got on his bike,
and set off again
along the bumpy track
toward the pond.

Splat's bike
went clickity clickity clack
clack clack.

Splat stopped by the pond
and opened his backpack.
Duck popped out,
looked about,
then popped back in again.

"Maybe Duck isn't lost," Splat said.

"Mrs. Wimpydimple

will know what to do."

And Splat wobbled his way

back on the track to Cat School.

When Splat got to school,
he parked his bike
in the bike-rack shack
and dropped his backpack
on the bumpy track.

Duck looked out from a crack
in Splat's backpack.
Duck saw Spike's silly grin
and had a panic attack.

Duck jumped out
of Splat's backpack.
"Duck! Duck!" yelled Splat.

"Where? Where?" yelled Plank,

looking blank.

Too late . . .

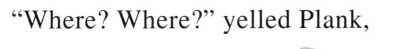

SPLURF!

The duck with the little book

sat on Plank's head.

"No quack!" said Splat.

"No quack?" asked Spike

"No quack?" asked Plank.

"No quack!" said Splat.

"A duck lacking in quacking,"

said Spike and Plank.

"That's not right."

"Maybe Duck is hungry," said Spike.

Spike took the fish-stick snack

from Splat's backpack

and gave it to Duck.

But Duck didn't bite.

So Spike ate the fish-stick

snack himself.

"Maybe Duck is sad and needs to be cheered up," said Plank. Plank made a funny face.

Duck didn't laugh.

Duck didn't even grin.

Plank's funny face stayed stuck.

"I know, I know!" said Kitten.

"Duck needs a bow

with a little pink dress to match.

That will bring Duck's quack back."

But the bow and the dress

were not a success.

Duck's beak stayed firmly closed.

"Mrs. Wimpydimple will know

what to do," said Splat.

Mrs. Wimpydimple looked at the duck.

"A duck lacking in quacking?"

she asked.

"How very odd.

But the answer must be simple,"

said Mrs. Wimpydimple.

"I will examine this duck
with the little book,"
said Mrs. Wimpydimple.
She played some music
to test Duck's ears.

Duck danced a merry duck dance.

"Duck's hearing is all right.

Maybe the problem

is Duck's eyesight,"

said Mrs. Wimpydimple.

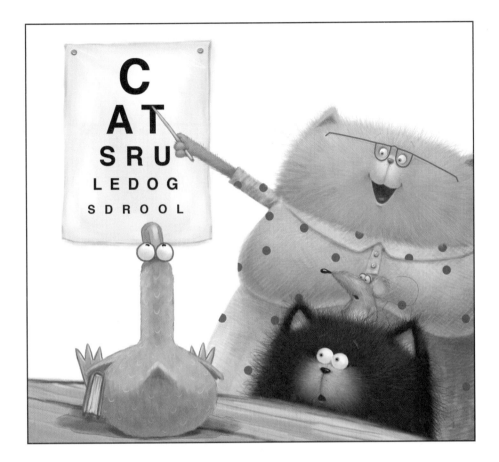

Mrs. Wimpydimple pointed to a chart.

Duck just looked blank.

She looked closely at Duck.

"Hmmm . . . I see," she said.

"But I don't think Duck does."

Mrs. Wimpydimple put her glasses
on Duck's beak.

Duck blinked.

Duck opened the book
and started to read out loud.

As he read, Duck began to quack.

"Quack . . . quack, quack . . ."

Followed by a "quack, quack, quack."

"Hooray for Duck!"

cheered the helpful cats.

Duck's quack was back.

And that was that.

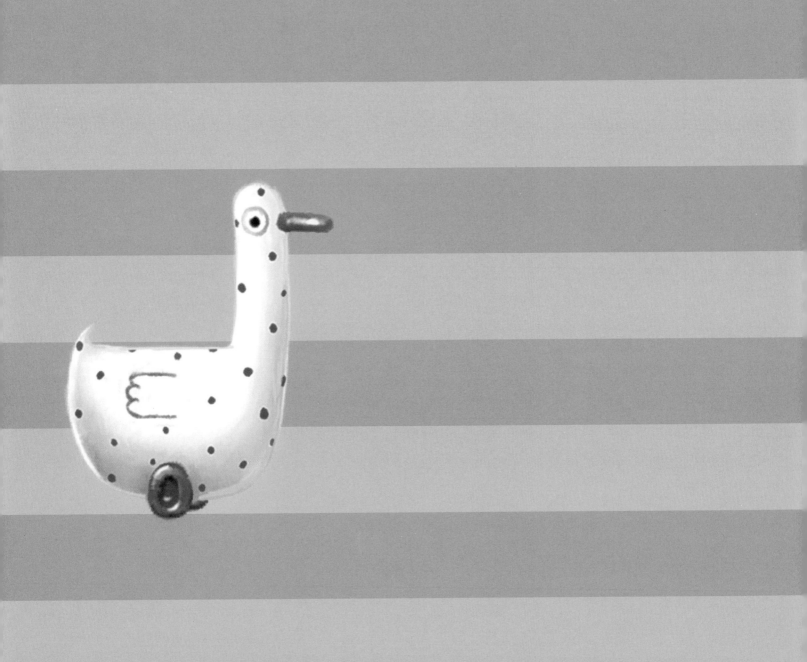

Splat the cat
sat watching *Super Cat* on TV.
It was his favorite show.

161

This time, brave Super Cat
was saving his tiny town
from an awful earthquake!

Splat said, "I want to be a
brave hero, too.
Eek! Look out—a snake!
Seymour, I'll save you!"

So Splat saved Seymour

from a sneaky snake.

But he forgot to beware

of his mango milkshake . . .

SPLAT!

"That's that!" exclaimed Dad.

"No more Super Cat.

No more TV."

Pfft!

"No more TV?" Splat groaned.

"No more TV!" said his mom.

"Why not take a bike ride to the lake?"

"Yes, I could use a break," said Splat.

Splat took off on his bike.

Riding helped him shake

his mango milkshake mistake.

On his way to the lake,

Splat saw a big sign.

A clever thought crossed his mind.

He could bake a TV-winning cake.

Splat never made it to the lake.

Instead, he sped home

to bake his cake.

He opened Mom's cake book

and looked and flipped.

But no cake in that book

had the tippy-top look

of a super first-prize cake.

So Splat said, "I'll bake

my own super-duper cake.

One that nobody else can make!"

Splat said, "Let's see.

I'll need a large pan or two,

or maybe three."

Splat put in

all the things he needed

to bake a super-duper cake.

Splat said to Seymour,

"More cake flour

makes more cake power!"

Then he added one more thing.

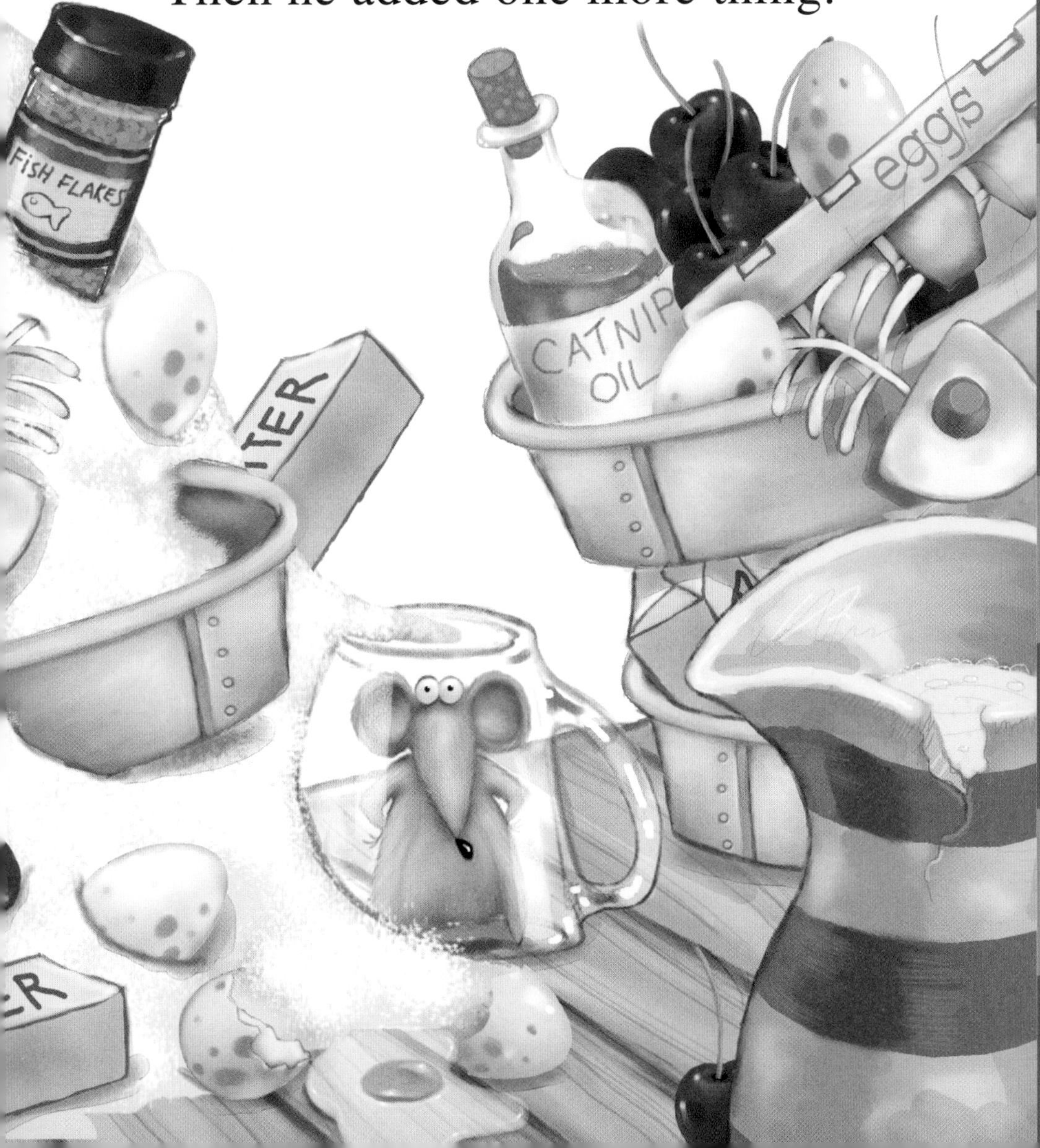

The cake was now ready to bake.
But that last thing Splat added
was a big, BIG mistake!

SPLAT!

Now there was no cake.

And there was a BIG mess.

Splat was too tired to bake
another cake.

He went to bed thinking,

"How will I win the TV?

What would Super Cat do?"

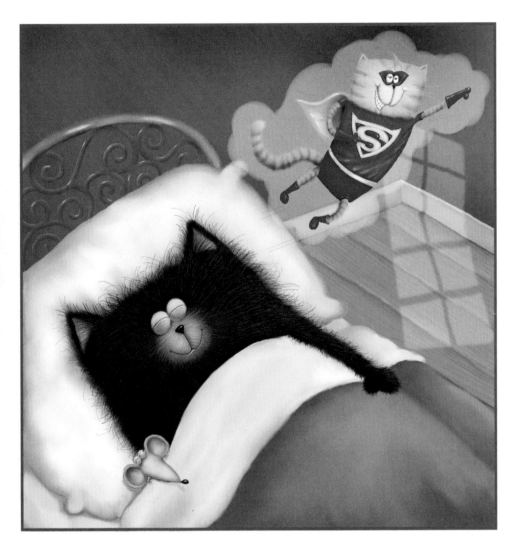

Then Splat dreamed
of Super Cat.

When Splat woke up
he knew what to do
and how to bake his super cake.

At the contest, Splat was ready.

Spike was there with his cake.

Kitten was there with her cake.

Plank had baked a cake, too.

Spike's cake was wider.

Kitten's cake was prettier.

Plank's cake was taller.

Was Splat's cake super enough?

SUPER CAT!

The judges looked closely
at every cake baked.
They tasted the cakes.
They talked together.

Then one judge said,

"Our top judge will now

award the Super Cake prize."

Surprise!

The top judge was really Super Cat!

"Splat the cat takes the cake!"

said Super Cat.

"I mean he takes the TV."

Splat was very happy.
When he got home
he said, "Now it's time
to watch *Super Cat*!"

"It's you who takes the cake,
Super Cat," whispered Splat.